Atheneum Books for Young Readers • An imprint of Simon & Schuster Children's Publishing Division • 1230 Avenue of the Americas, New York, New York 10020 • Text copyright © 2003 by Jeanne Willis • Illustrations copyright © 2003 by Tony Ross • First published in Great Britain in 2003 by Andersen Press Ltd. • First U.S. edition, 2005 • All rights reserved, including the right of reproduction in whole or in part in any form. • The text for this book is set in Garamond Infant. • The illustrations for this book are rendered in pen, ink, and watercolor. • Manufactured in Italy • 10 9 8 7 6 5 4 3 2 1 • Library of Congress Cataloging-in-Publication Data • Willis, Jeanne. • Tadpole's promise / Jeanne Willis ; illustrated by Tony Ross.— 1st American ed. • p. cm. • "An Anne Schwartz Book." • Summary: When a caterpillar meets her perfect love, a tadpole, she begs him never to change, but their relationship is doomed. • ISBN 0-689-86524-4 • [1. Tadpoles—Fiction. 2. Caterpillars—Fiction. 3. Metamorphosis—Fiction.] I. Ross, Tony, ill. II. Title. • PZ7.W68313Tad 2005 • [E]—dc22 • 2004011502

jeanne willis  tony ross

Tadpole's promise

AN ANNE SCHWARTZ BOOK

Atheneum Books for Young Readers

NEW YORK LONDON TORONTO SYDNEY

Where the willow meets the water,
a tadpole met a caterpillar.
They gazed into each other's tiny eyes . . .

and fell in love.
She was his beautiful rainbow,

and he was her shiny black pearl.
"I love everything about you,"
said the tadpole.

"I love everything about you," said the caterpillar. "Promise you'll never change."

"I promise," he said.

But as sure as the weather changes,
the tadpole could not keep his promise.
Next time they met, he had grown two legs.

"You've broken your promise,"
                        said the caterpillar.

"Forgive me," begged the tadpole.
"I couldn't help it. I don't want these legs. . . .

All I want is my beautiful rainbow."

"All I want is my shiny black pearl.
Promise me you'll never change,"
said the caterpillar.

"I promise," he said.

But sure as the seasons change,
the next time they met,
he had grown arms.

"That's twice you've broken your promise," cried the caterpillar.

"Forgive me," begged the tadpole. "I could not help it.
I do not want these arms. . . .

All I want is my beautiful rainbow."

"And all I want is my shiny black pearl.
I will give you one last chance,"
said the caterpillar.

But as surely as the world changes,
the tadpole could not keep his promise.
The next time they met,
he had no tail.

"You have broken your promise three times,
and now you have broken my heart,"
said the caterpillar.

"But you are my beautiful rainbow,"
said the tadpole.

"Yes, but you are not my shiny black pearl.
Good-bye."

She crawled up the willow branch
and cried herself to sleep.

One warm moonlit night,
she woke up.
The sky had changed.
The trees had changed.
Everything had changed . . .

except for her love for the tadpole. Even though he'd broken his promise, she decided to forgive him.

She dried her wings
and fluttered down to look for him.

Where the willow meets the water,
a frog was sitting on a lily pad.

"Excuse me," she said.
"Have you seen my shiny black . . ."

But faster than she could say "pearl,"
the frog leapt up and swallowed her

in one great gulp.

And there he waits . . .

thinking fondly of his beautiful rainbow . . .

. . . wondering where she went.

THE END